MW01639567

Pilot Light

William Ashbless
Tim Powers
James P. Blaylock

Subterranean Press 2008

First Edition

ISBN
978-1-59606-141-5

Subterranean Press
PO Box 190106
Burton, MI 48519

www.subterraneanpress.com

Table of Contents

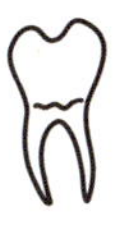

introduction

by Tim Powers

It has been more than five years now since William Ashbless drove off in my 1981 Ford pickup truck to find the legended Gate to Hell in Tull, Kansas. The ruined walls of the 130-year-old Evangelical Emmanuel Church, behind which the gate was rumored to stand, were torn down in March of 2002, about the time Ashbless would have arrived there—very shortly after his arrival is my guess. The only message, if you can call it that, which we got from him was a post-card, mailed from Kansas City in March, 2002—on the front was printed half-a-dozen grotesque laughing faces and the legend, "This is the kind of time we had in ...," and someone, presumably Ashbless, had written "K. C." in pencil in the blank space. There was no message on the reverse side.

My truck, which he had promised to return within the month, has not reappeared.

Almost a year earlier, in May of 2001, he had borrowed money from James Blaylock and myself to fly to Israel, where he hoped to find a gate to Hell in the valley of Gehenna, outside the walls of Jerusalem. There he dug holes, shuffled around with a dowsing rod, scattered copper pennies on the grass to see which ones, if any, would turn black, and borrowed more money from one Naomi Wiener, a young lady who admired the poetry he claimed to have written—but he failed to find a gate, and flew back in defeat to the United States. It remained for Blaylock and I to repay Miss Wiener.

Authorities in Tull are unwilling to speak at any length about Ashbless's probable visit to their town, and a "John Doe" corpse that was found not all that far from the old church some time after Ashbless would have arrived was cremated before Blaylock and I began to wonder what had become of the old poet. Shrewd scholars will not be slow in coming to conclusions.

introduction

Ashbless always described himself as a writer—in spite of the fact that he seemed to make his meager living entirely by buying stuffed animals at thrift stores and selling them on Ebay—and among his effects Blaylock and I found the soiled typescripts of several short stories that he had written back in the 1960s. The best of these is the effort that follows this introduction, "Pilot Light," which he apparently intended to submit to Harlan Ellison for Ellison's anthology, *Dangerous Visions*. If Ashbless did indeed send the story to Ellison, Ellison's reply does not survive, and the story did not appear in the anthology. Open-minded readers are invited to imagine that Ashbless did not actually send it, and that Ellison would have bought it if he had, and that the story would thus by now have derived at least some associational importance.

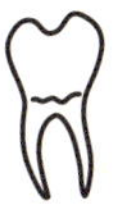

postscript to the introduction

As readers of *Locus* magazine will by now already know, our melancholy speculations that Ashbless had died have once again proven to be groundless. It goes without saying that we're all overjoyed to learn this, though I've had to pay a substantial amount to get my truck out of an impound yard in Clark County, Nevada. The text of this book had already been extensively proof-read by the time he appeared, penniless and "ill," last month in Long Beach, and then disappeared again, only to turn up in Hawaiian Gardens, and so it was not feasible to extend him any special editing privileges, but the publisher has generously allowed him to annotate the text with footnotes. We're assured that these will be brief, succinct, and useful to the reader in exploring the many levels of this story.

Tim Powers
Muscoy, California
June 22, 2007

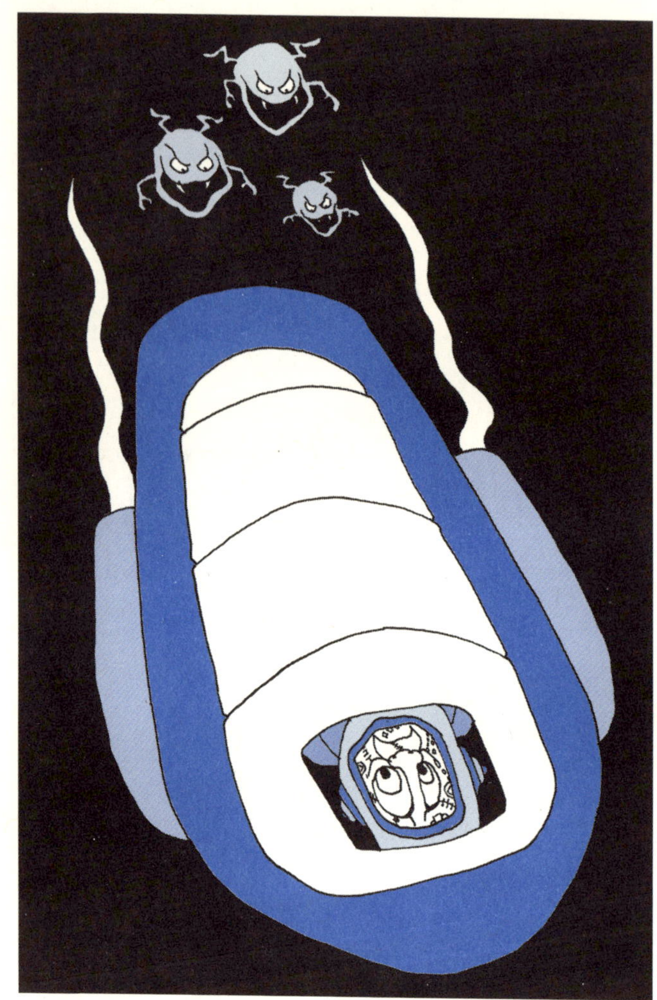

pilot light

by William Ashbless

"There is no rest for a messenger until the message is delivered."

—Joseph Conrad,

The Rescue

It glided, wheeling, above me—salvation, it was, but unreachable to me. I was as compressed by gravity as if I were sat upon by apostate Atlas, and tears plummeted back over my sagging cheeks and pinged a soft tattoo on the taut metal of the bulkhead. All I could move was myeyeballs, which were trying to burrow backward into the yielding memory pudding of my brain. Discomfiting—but not half as discomfiting as the face that peered through a sort of vent near the port side of my head, grimaced, and disappeared. Before my brain could consider that spectral visitation, one of my front teeth snapped clean off and shot back into my throat, choking me.

> "Everything, saith Epictetus, hath two handles, —the one to be held by, the other not."
>
> —Robert Burton,
> *The Anatomy of Melancholy*

I had never wound it so tightly—double bumps all down the line—and I was afraid the rubber band would break.[1]

Crouching on the grass, I leaped up high in my new Keds and let the plane go.

---

1 For the record, I myself was the inventor of the rubber-band glider, although another man took credit for it, and I never saw a dime of royalty money. I filed the papers with a clerk at the patent office named Warburton, who failed to process the schemata, and then quit, waited two years, and filed it as his own, and it's his name you'll see on the patent today, and not the name Ashbless. Warburton's a rich man now, living on his unholy gain in New Jersey, and I'm living out here in Hawaiian Gardens in a dump.

God's onion[2] splendor in an ounce of flimsy balsa wood, it arced and soared up into the dizzying sky, disappearing, burning out of sight in the great white, blinding eye of the sun....

I waited, grounded, for the thing to fall back into view and crack, as it generally did, against a tree limb or curbside and splinter to pieces. I could always fix

---

2 I don't have access to the original manuscript here, because Powers and Blaylock absconded with it and then sold it, but it seems to me that "onion" might be a misprint. It's been forty years – My God, closer to fifty! – since I wrote the piece, and so I can't confirm the onion or deny it. A literary critic might read it as metaphor, like in the vegetable poem by what's-his-name, but then a literary critic reads his newspaper and thinks that Wheeling, West Virginia, is an engineering project, to take the first example that comes to mind. Still and all, we can make a case for the onion here, and I'll let it stand. (The contract between Subterranean Press and Powers and Blaylock prevents me from changing the text, which is why I have to tread lightly with these annotations if I want to collect the fifty dollars that Mr. Schaffer promised me, and which I haven't seen yet. I can use that fifty.)

them, though, my balsa wood gliders, and after a few dozen flights this particular craft was so patched, repaired, and re-glued that almost none of the original plane remained, and it was a living example of the great Myth of Permanent Patchability, in which I have always passionately believed, even in the face of...

And so I waited... and I waited... seeing faces in the clouds—God's visage among them? Colonel Wick?[3]—and the afternoon sun wavered and melted into the sea, and the moon and stars arose in the heavens and fled through the wheeling darkness as if on the current of a savage wind, and, it seems to me now, I waited forever until forever passed before me along with the rest of it, but without my pilotless glider.

"Look at my bald head! Hark! Listen, ye serpents, listen!"

—William Blake,
Tiriel, I:28[4]

---

3 Not Wick. I know that now.

4 Blake was a real corker, and most people didn't know him

as well as they *thought* they did, but that's a whole nother story, as old Phebus the gardener used to say, usually when he was drunk, which he generally was by about nine in the morning, and on whiskey, too. The man had an ironclad stomach, for a shrub-cutter. Blake made use of him, by the way, in his little-read science fiction story "An Island in the Moon," chapter the third, where he's introduced as the god of Cookery, among other things. Those of you who read my cookbook might be surprised to hear that it was old Phebus Larson who taught me the Fundamentals, but about that I can't say more. I'm not here to solve mysteries, but to comment on this story. (Phebus's common-law wife, Hettie Gimblet figures in Blake's piece, too, and is mentioned in Chapter 1 as a toper of the first water – although it's pretty certain that water never crossed her lips after the age of three, and in fact when she died, her corpse didn't show any sign of decomposition for nearly three weeks, because it was so steeped in alcohol.) Blake, as you know, was quoting Second Kings, verse 23, in an upside down way. He'd heard the cry, "Go up, thou baldhead" more than once himself, and he was fixing to call out the bears on a crowd of punks that used to lounge around on the sidewalk over in the Seven Dials where Blake

"**He's in functional** condition? You're certain?"

I was always chagrined when they talked as if

---

spent some time living in a sewer-side hovel owned by that son of a bitch Carwell (who met Karma coming around the back side of the barn one night, and don't we wish we had a snapshot of the look on his face?) Harold Bloom pointed out that in Blake's poetry, "The Vehicular Form is the outward circumference of an individual energy," but if you ask me the idea's specious. I have no regard for the Vehicular Form, and you can't bring it to bear on "The Island in the Moon" without opening a can of worms, although Bloom himself is a good man, and is right more often than he's wrong. I can't say fairer than that. One thing you might not know – almost no one does, except me and a couple of party-colored devils who found out the hard way – is that Bethel, the ancient city wherefrom the old Baldhead descended, is twelve miles outside of Jerusalem, due north, and it was burnt to a cinder in B.C. 1400. The mountains thereabout are a warren of caves, several of which link Bethel to the Valley of Gehenna, or "The Lake of Fire": "The Beast and the False Prophet still exist there, undestroyed." So sayeth the Book of Revelations. "Go up thou Baldhead" indeed…

I were a piece of repaired machinery sitting on the deck, incapable of hearing.

"Certain, sir. The Army Surplus liver has taken root firmly, and the peritoneum is knitting, after a fashion.[5] The teeth are loose yet, but he doesn't eat very often. No, I think you could put him into field operation immediately."

The sturgeon[6] stuffed his papers into a briefcase

5 There's a few things I could tell you about the Organ Bank out at Fort Dix – what they call the "Second Commissary," but I won't. What rough beast…? There are things that aren't safe for a civilian to know.

6 Clearly the word is "surgeon" here and not "sturgeon" for the love of Mike. I don't know who Subterranean Press is hiring to illustrate this story, but by God if there's a picture of a fish in it I'm going to clean someone's plow. What most people don't know about me is that I had a career as an amateur boxer back in the day, and I mean the *day*, and I went 43 rounds with the Game Chicken in the yard of the Portsmouth Dragon and made the Chicken wish he'd stayed home. You can take that as gospel, and if you take it as a warning you can take it to the bank.

and, after saluting, left the room.

Colonel Wick cocked an eyebrow at me. "Sikorski," he said curiously, "are there any of your original parts left?"

I considered it, unconsciously stroking the scar tissue on my face. "I don't know, sir. I think the left knee-cap is part of the original package." I shrugged. "I could be wrong."

"You're a game one, Sikorski, a game one. But if this occurs one more time..." He shook his head. I waited for his curious and inevitable warning. I'd heard it before, but it had become no less mystifying. "Once more," Wick said, "and you'll wake up with two heads and both feet growing from your mouth. Your liver all bollixed up! You wouldn't like that, boy. You wouldn't like that. You wouldn't like... Two heads! Feet! Liver! Two feet-heads! Liver!"

I managed to lift myself off the cot high enough to punch poor old Wick on the shoulder. He closed down, eyes tumbling shut like one of these dolls that you tilt one way and the other to wake them up and put them to sleep. The very sound of the word "liver" had become an abomination to me.

I coughed like a trumped-up[7] bellows, shooting the tooth (a calcium bullet!) through the phantom Captain Wick, blown up like a balloon out of the dresser-drawer of my memory.

Ptoo! Whish! Gone.

"Life and art and love and duty,
Ah, there, sweet cutie."
—H. P. Lovecraft

Again the face peers in at me. Where have I seen it before? It was…

It was…

---

7 Damn it! This is supposed to be *tromped-on*. What the hell is a "trumped-up" bellows supposed to be? A God-damned, stinking piece of lunacy, that's what. For God's sake they could have got a chimpanzee to transcribe this story and saved their money! This is what they call dip-shittery out here in Hawaiian Gardens, but I'm prevented by contract from making it right!

It was a hot-wind night in Coney Island, lit like a Bosch hell by whirling, skeletal, colored lights on fright rides.

I was on the spinning-planes ride, pinned to the Coke-sticky seat by centrifugal force. I turned to Marge, thinking of a quick kiss… but it wasn't Marge's face that turned toward mine.[8]

It was… another face. Wizened and strangely winking.

And now, years later, it's here.

---

8 The less said about poor Marge, the better, I guess, but I'll point out that she was the love of my life, and since she… went away… I've lived alone, and it's a tough nut to reread this after so many years and to recollect that night at Coney Island and where it led. Let sleeping dogs lie, I suppose, especially if they're the hounds of your own personal Hell. And speaking of Hell, I intended to lean on that image of the Bosch Hell, which was meant to have *implications*, but maybe I wasn't forthright enough. I'm a man who values artistic subtlety, but some of us remember what Toby Smollett used to say about "a virtue over-toasted." (See footnote 4.)

"For a' that, and a' that,
An' twice as muckle's a' that."
—Robert Burns
The Jolly Beggars

Pursuit—that's what I call it. But it's not the first, nor, I pray, the last, nor yet the myth of pursuit (a lower-case myth in that gravity-laden whirlybird flight) but some sense of pursuit that no dictionary has embraced. The acceleration was dropping off; that was fairly clear, thank God. I managed to drag one leg around and, raising a leaden arm, pried against the louvers. The face was there again, eyes wide as the sea, mouth like a prefabricated tool-shed.[9] I started to exclaim, but the face was gone on the instant— *puffo*, like the magician's coin —and it seemed for a moment, for an imperceptible slice of time, that a tiny, whirring wooden glider bobbed and hovered and wisped away into nothing, into the now-eyeless, empty, louvered

9 Jung is your man for this one.

vent in the core of an off-worlder, bound for the Centauri System.

I was a messenger, but I never asked myself what the message was. Probably something filthy.

"O flesh, flesh, how art thou fishified!"
—William Shakespeare,
Romeo and Juliet, Act II,scene IV

The Alphans had *put me through a battery of narco-hypnotic tests and interrogations, and for the next few weeks I tossed on my metal acceleration couch shaken by vivid dreams as an old shoe is shaken by a dog....*

"I still worry about their catching him."

"You're paid to worry. This is set to failsafe. First, he doesn't know what the message is; second, he doesn't even consciously think of himself as a messenger. One tiny cluster of coded molecules in his pelvis![10] How likely are they to find

10 For the record: hip.

that? And of course even if they somehow do, there's the low-yield plutonium charge in his liver. Those boys start messing around and there'll be nothing left of our lad Sikorski but a cloud of incandescent fog...."

> "When breath blew back,
> And on the other side
> I heard recede the disappointed tide!"
> —Emily Dickinson

The hammer. The flipping hammer—a Coney Island horror. I'd been sick. Hot dog and relish and a quart of beer and I parting company around that last loop. Marge, skeletal beneath the arc lights, laughed through steel teeth at my misery. "Surely," I said, "surely this... this!" and she congealed once again, shoulders plump and glistening. We shot away, it seemed, toward the heavens, and I heard the whirring, and the sound of an over-laden rubber band thumping as it unwound....

"A sleveless errand."
—John Heywood,
Proverbes

Hatcha-ka-wa, hatcha-ka-wa, hatcha! Hatcha! Something didn't sound right. Those extra gees had hashed up more than a few ribs.

Once the toy plane had dived headfirst into a briar bush.

"That's hashed up more than a wing-edge or two!" yelped my brother as we loped down the grassy hill.

A gang of little boys had glimpsed the falling plane, and ran toward the bushes. "*Hatcha-ka-wa*!" they cawed, waving sticks.

"You've got to get the thing before they do," gasped Colonel Wick, running and leaping beside me, "or there won't be any of it left."

Except a kneecap, I thought.[11]

---

11 But *which* kneecap? I think I specified, in the original manuscript, and Blaylock and Powers just arrogantly trimmed it. As an

"For May wol have no slogardye a-night.
The sesoun priketh every gentil herte,
And maketh him out of his sleep to sterte."
—Geoffrey Chaucer,
The Canterbury Tales

There he is again! Why won't he speak, why won't he explain why he replaced Marge for one infernal instant in Coney Island, so long ago?

Hah! That tooth ludicrously imbedded in the pale forehead. None of us is presentable anymore.

But can I be certain? Is this quest my onion[12], or another's? And what of Colonel Wick and the

---

unregarded detail, I consider the distinction important.

12 Here it is again! And again I can't swear to the onion, but it's true that there's an element of autobiography in this story, and the reference to the salad at Bernardo's calls up memories of red onions and pepperocinis that I can swear to, and so once again I'll let the onion stand. It's a plausible figure, maybe even artistic, but I'll admit that it makes me nervous, and I'm beginning suspect the hand of Blaylock here, taking liberties.

salad bowl at Bernardo's that night on the midway? Mambrino's Helmet[13] or a salad bowl? "Midway down the midway," she had said cryptically.

> "He made him a hut, wherein he did put
> The carcass of Robinson Crusoe.
> O poor Robinson Crusoe!"[14]
>
> —Samuel Foote,
> *The Mayor of Garrett*, Act I, scene I

"And soldier!"

"Yup!"

"We none of us will come up for a third time save Skorski, or Skinki, or what-the-hell."

---

13 The reference, of course, is to Mambrino's *actual* helmet (not Quixote's barber's basin) which surfaced in Barcelona in the 17th Century and was carried out to Constantinople two years later decorated as a fruit bowl. Where is it now? More than one of us would like an answer to that one, although I have my suspicions. Istanbul? – or shifted elsewhere?

14 And of course we know that he *did* "make him a hut."

"Yup!"

"What the hell is it?"

"Sikorski, sir. Yup!"

"That boy's a patch-work quilt with a propeller nose, blastin' off again and again. But he was always a clean liver!" Colonel Wick sputtered out behind the slats.

"Who's loony now?"

—John Armstrong Chaloner, 1911

In the end we're alone. In the end I'm alone.

Choose one, but don't show it to me.

Don't show anything to me.

Get out of here.

It/We/You has failed. The Alphans let me go, finally, but they must have messed with the guidance system—I'm off course, and acceleration is simply going up steadily.[15] Already I'm immobilized

15 The use of the phrase "off course" was dicey here for a couple of reasons, although the weather of the passing years, I suppose, has worn away any problem with the mere revelation

in the acceleration couch. The Brussard ramjet will try for all eternity to attain c, but soon I'll implode under the g-forces and then be an unrippled red pool, islanded in geometric patterns by the tread-corrugations of the steel floor, until the corrugations themselves collapse.

("Not the beach, Marge. Red tide this week."

Colonel Wick kisses me, greasing my cheek with lipstick. "But I've already bought the *suntan oil*.")

Will the cluster of coded molecules in my pelvis be broken beyond restoration before any sentience finds my ship? Perhaps we will reach c, in spite of Einstein, and it will be God who is stuck with reconstructing the message. Wasn't that a dainty dish to set before a King?

But for now all I can see is Colonel Wick's pale face, filtering backward through my memories like that dye for microscope slides that turns certain things blue.

---

of the *fact*. I ask my readers not to try to read "off course" as any kind of personal statement, which it isn't.

He changes certain faces into his onion[16] while

16 Damn it! His *onion*? What did Chesterton say about this kind of thing? You see something as ridiculous as a human nose, and it seems like it must be a mistake. Then you see another one, on another face, and it raises your suspicions, but you write it off as coincidence. Then you see a *third* nose, and you're by-God certain it's a plot. That's the kind of thing we've got here. What the hell kind of monkey-brained idiots transcribed this story? Oh, Powers and Blaylock! Shoot-hell! *Pardon* me for defaming the monkey! The word had to have been "own," and not "onion," and I'd appreciate it if you'd read it that way. We'll keep those first two onions or not, but we'll throw this one into the garbage, because it's a by-God rotten onion if it's an onion at all. Was this an honest mistake? Were Powers and Blaylock so bound up in the idea of onions as metaphors, that they began to find them under every bush? Perhaps they didn't mean anything by it, you say. Or perhaps they're the scum-sucking pigs that I *think* they are. And speaking of onions and things that stink, let me tell you a little something that they'd rather I kept quiet. Fifteen years ago, when those two clowns were in need of ready money that they couldn't steal out of their wives'

purses, they took day jobs with Waste Management out there in Orange, driving trash trucks – those new ones with the big pincers that pick up the barrel wholesale and dump it upside down over the top of the truck. I don't know who was working the pincers, and I suppose it's six of one and half dozen of the other, but one of them picked up an old lady who was emptying her garbage at the last moment and *dumped her into the hopper.* Apparently she shouted pretty loud, and a neighbor spotted her just as the pincers let her go and she fell into the trash, and he managed to stop the truck and convey to the two fools that this woman was trapped inside. You wouldn't guess what they did. That's right, they abandoned the truck and ran off. They high-tailed it. The way the neighbor tells it, they got halfway down the alley, and then Blaylock figured out that he'd left his lunchbox in the cab of the truck, and *he went back after it*, the cheap skink. The neighbor had already climbed in over the top, and was lowering himself into the bin to haul out the victim, and so it was too late to confront Blaylock there on the street. Otherwise, this neighbor tells me, there'd have been blood on the asphalt. What happened is that the old lady survived, but they had to hose her down with tomato juice to

I'm not looking, and when I review my memories, there he is.

I'm glad there's no mirror visible from here.

I know whose face, tortured bulbous grimacing face with a tooth planted in the forehead, I'd see.

But all reactions need their catalysts, all combustive machines their pilot light. Even a paraffin candle needs a wick before it burns.

---

get rid of the smell, like they do when a person gets sprayed by a skunk. This is all in the police log out there in Orange, by the way. Powers and Blaylock were charged with misdemeanor battery and leaving the scene of an accident, and they had to do 200 community service hours over at the St. Vincent de Paul warehouse, where they sorted mattresses, which led to a fire that liked to have burned down the whole shebang when Powers lost hold of a lit cigarette. They ran off again and later denied it all, and of course the cigarette burned along with the mattresses, and so there was no DNA evidence, and the two of them got off scot free after putting in about two and a half hours. Let them sue me if I'm wrong about any of this.

And what of me?[17] If I could just get up, get these damn fingers through the slats there in the port side of my head… If I could just grope about in that dark Wick-bewitched grotto, peer down that black midway along the dark, Coney Island night, I could see, I think I *do* see, a phantom, flat-winged, slat-bodied, red-propellered rubber-band glider, still sailing and sailing and sailing.[18]

---

17 For God's sake, don't look to Blaylock and Powers for an answer to this one. Physician, heal thyself!

18 I *remember* that I ended this story with a long passage of blank verse, which Powers and Blaylock have high-handedly chosen to omit. Powers swears the manuscript ended as you see it here, and speculates cravenly that there might have been a last page that got lost. That old gag. The poem went, roughly:

"[da-dum, da-dum] in bleak oblivion's sky,
Where nevermore can [dum da-dum da-dum]
Nor earthbound lovers scan the—"

Never mind, never mind. Vandals!

afterword: a brief clarification of william ashbless's "Pilot Light"

by James Blaylock

The height of William Ashbless's perch in the towering pantheon of post-modern writers hasn't been clearly established, except perhaps by the poet himself, when he uttered his now-infamous bon mot in the *Paris Review* "chat" nearly three decades ago: "The view is good from up here."

Not everyone has shared his view of the view. Jacques Derrida (I can safely reveal, now that both men have passed away) wrote a highly interesting, lengthy treatise on Asbless (something that will come as a surprise to many of you, who haven't—and couldn't have—read it) entitled "The Literary Rigors of a Marine Coelacanth." We know two things: that Asbless somehow got hold of the Derrida paper a month before it was slated for publication, and that the paper was suppressed when the President of the Modern Language Association found his car wrecked in a ditch off the Garden State Parkway in New Jersey, about two miles up from the Highway 72 turnoff. The back seat was filled with dead sardines, among which was buried one of Ashbless's "business" cards. Were the fish a *message*? When word got back to Derrida, he read the sardines in just that way despite his contempt for clear, particular interpretations of language and image, and he withdrew the paper, famously suggesting that, "A heap of dead fish are a text every bit as readable as a heap of foolscap."

"Theory," Dr. Johnson tells us, "shall have little influence on practice." Unlike Freud's cigar (or perhaps it was Kipling's cigar) sometimes a dead fish is *not* just a dead fish, and a sardine is as good as a smoke!

My contention, however, is that Ashbless might have overreacted to the fish reference in Derrida's title, and that the withdrawal of the paper was premature. Derrida, I mean to say, quite likely didn't intend for the title to cast a pejorative shadow over the poet's career. That the marine coelacanth is a relic of the Devonian Age is inarguable, and Ashbless would naturally bristle at the very idea of he or his poetry being considered relics of *any* age. But the marine coelacanth, I'll remind you, was considered extinct for thousands of years before *reappearing* in a fisherman's net off Madagascar in the 20th Century. Ashbless, we scarcely need mention, has himself been associated with a number of impossible reappearances (not to mention impossible fish). My point is that there are two ways to look at a marine coelacanth (as Epictetus and Robert Burton remind us. And tell me: why that *particular* quotation, given that Burton was a master of epigram? What "handle" had we best not hold? And we're reminded by Shakespeare of old Henry's sage advice to Prince Hal—that he had best drink from the *near* side of his tankard, for it he dare drink from the *far* side, he would assuredly "suffer an ale-soaked tunic"!)

(And to avoid putting too fine a point on the matter, I won't delve into my own allusions to the subject of fishy reappearances, but I will say that I made literary use of the theme in a book I wrote in the 1980s, a book in which Ashbless put in an appearance. Its publication was followed closely by the theft of a Chevy pickup truck I owned at the time, *which was abandoned axle-deep in water out in Trabuco Canyon with six dead trout in the bed*. Did the trout *leap* into the truck, perhaps mistaking the bed of the truck for the bed of the river?)

We see the fish theme carried through elsewhere in the story. The "sturgeon" is particularly interesting, especially the fact that there's no previous reference at all to a sturgeon (let alone an ambulatory sturgeon) being in the room with our destroyed protagonist. The sturgeon appears in the story *merely to exit the story*—Godot appearing at long last, like God out of a machine, not to take part, *but to take his leave?*—a touch of that post-modern, perhaps unconscious, brilliance that arises in Ashbless's work like a discordant but compelling phrase surfacing and resurfacing in a piece of music. And of course there's Wick, always Wick, sometimes a phantom, "sputtering out behind the slats" and then re-igniting, like one of those birthday candles that you buy in a joke shop. It is in Wick, the sometime-phantom, that the "riverrun, past Eve and Adam's," carries us on its billows to perhaps the most memorable passage in all of Joyce's *Finnegans Wake*: "But there's leps of flam in Funnycoon's Wick...." Did Ashbless scruple against borrowing from Joyce? Apparently not, for at least by implication there are "leps of flam" in Ashbless's Wick as well, enervating and energizing in equal measure.

(If one looks south, the story perhaps didn't want or need the quotation from Shakespeare, because it had already been "fishified" by the sturgeon. Ushering in the Bard appears at a hasty glance to be mere countersinking. But on the other hand, as Ashbless himself was likely to say, are five fingers, and one of them points due north. Again we turn to Burton and Epictetus, and to Ashbless's own ramblings about the drowning of his lamented father, who "sleeps with the fishes, but uneasily." Indeed, "full fathom five" his father lies, "fishified," and of course Joyce's deadsea dugong "updipdripping from the depths" comes to mind immediately. Ashbless's sturgeon, we discover, is a slippery eel, and just when it seems we've deconstructed him, and at last we're looking at his liver and lights, he slips back into the river of text and disappears into the shadows. If we're searching for sheer literary brilliance in this odd story, we find it in the character of the sturgeon.)

On a different note, I'll point out that it would be impossible to read "Pilot Light" sensibly without an understanding of the metaphorical implications of the "onion" which appears in disconcerting ways no fewer than three times in the text. The figure isn't a difficult one: consider the easily-generated tears, the peeling away of paper skin and then the layers of flesh beneath, like the psyche sloughing off layers of fabricated persona, revealing *what* at the center?—an edible core that's perhaps the most toothsome part of the fruit (one can hardly refer to an onion as a root!) or a rotted bit of pith, which, like the accidentally-punctured liver of the blowfish, has permeated the whole with its decay? (We envision the "apostate Atlas" bent beneath the weight of an Olympian onion.) That image, of course—the layers within layers—*must* be read as an indirect allusion to the sturgeon's "briefcase" which contains, brilliantly... *we know not what.*

Fish and onions! Ashbless wouldn't have gone far wrong had he titled the piece "Bouillabaisse" in the manner of Guy de Maupassant. And of course I mean that in the most profoundly salutary way. Mr. Powers has informed us in his Introduction that Ashbless has passed on, and it's a sad business to write what is assuredly the first critical discussion and assessment of "Pilot Light" after the author's death. I'm convinced (to hearken back to the beginning of this piece) that it won't be the last such discussion, and that one day the clouds will part, and the literary stature of the old poet will be as conspicuous to us as the peak of Parnassus.

To the late lamented Ashbless I tip my hat and say, in the manner of Heywood, that his errand was not "sleveless." And I turn once again to a verse from

Ashbless's beloved Robert Burns, and "The Jolly Beggar"...

"A fairy fiddler frae the neuk
He skirl'd out, encore!"

Jim Blaylock
Orange, California
June 20, 2007

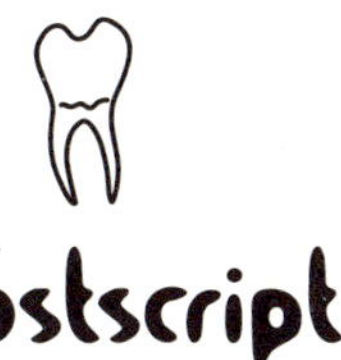

a postscript

by William Ashbless

And so I'm to have the "postscript" as a kindness. They might as well have given me a posthole digger, because the cemetery where Powers and Blaylock keep trying to plant me is so full of "John Doe" corpses by now that a man's got to be buried vertically if he's going to find any room at the inn. That conflagration out in Tull, Kansas, wasn't any kind of wienie roast, I can tell you that much, and Powers's truck wanted a little paint by the time the smoke cleared, but it was nothing that Wally's Paint and Body Shop couldn't have put right, and if Powers and Blaylock had treated me decently in this publication I'd have had the money to get the job done instead of the truck's ending up in that impound yard.

They tell me that Blaylock's got a job at the university, "teaching," and that he's banking on his little piece here to promote him to some kind of tenure. When I was annotating my story for Mr. Schafer at Subterranean Press, I pretty much gave the transcription the benefit of the doubt. (Powers and Blaylock, you'll remember, have the original manuscript, or *had* it, so I didn't have much choice in the matter.) I was skeptical of those onions, but I didn't want to make accusations—not at first. But as you know, if you've read the piece by now, I couldn't swallow that sturgeon no matter how it was filleted and fried. A tub of tartar sauce wouldn't answer. And now that I've read the galley proofs I see the lay of the land. Blaylock, I'm telling you, *loaded up my story with fish and onions in order to have something of his own to say.* A literary critic is a sad, damned, bloated creature, like Nebuchadnezzar down there on all fours eating hay, generating methane gas and doing a land-office business over at the university.

So I'm drawing out. I don't have many chips left on the table, and I'm out here in Hawaiian Gardens living in Miss Sessions' garage while a hazmat team cleans out my place in Long Beach, which was padlocked after Blaylock and Powers "fumigated" it as a favor to me, allegedly to get rid of termites. What the hell they were actually up to is a mystery, and for the sake of our sanity, it's a mystery that should remain unsolved. Like I say, I'm out of their penny-ante game for good and all. There's no point in driving out to Orange or Muscoy in order to poke the two of them in the eye again. I've talked reason to them, and I've tanned their hides with a bamboo whangee, but I might as well have been shooting peas into a can for all the good it did them or me. I'm quit of them.

Special
Bonus Feature

an interview with William Ashbless

by Bill Wylie

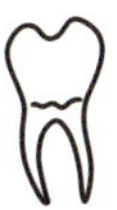

an interview

with William Ashbless

Publisher's Note:

What follows is a fragmentary interview of William Ashbless conducted recently by cub reporter Bill Wylie in Long Beach, California. The interview was never completed—our present text was mostly transcribed from a digital recording, and we've made every effort to reproduce meaningful vocalizations and nuances even when the recording was slightly unclear. (We note this because, in his annotations to the text of "Pilot Light" and in his comments afterward, Mr. Ashbless was slightly critical of the transcription of the manuscript, which, frankly, was stained with years of spilled liquids and foodstuffs, not to mention the problem of the poet's notoriously quirky handwriting, which can appear downright schizophrenic at times.) Suffice it to say that what you read here is our best attempt at a verbatim reproduction.

Now a small bit of recent history:

Subsequent to the "interview" (according to reporter Bill Wylie) William Ashbless asked to borrow forty dollars "for gas money down to Dago" which Mr. Wylie assumed meant the city of San Diego, a hundred miles to the south, very near the Mexican border. "It was all the money I had at the time," Wylie told the editors at Subterranean Press, "but Mr. Ashbless told me that he had to pay a visit to his 'poor old mother,' and under those sad circumstances I was happy to lend it to him." (Ashbless's "poor old mother"—if the poet is telling the truth about his own great age—must be upward of 280 years old. And nowhere is there any mention of Ashbless having family in San Diego.)

Ashbless has since disappeared, and, according to Ida Sessions of Hawaiian Gardens (who may have been inebriated when we first contacted her) the poet had moved out of his temporary quarters in her garage two days before this interview was conducted, after cautioning her, bafflingly, to be on the lookout for "a small man with a face like a road apple." Ashbless, she said, seemed to be in a state of some agitation. "You'd do me a favor," he allegedly told her, handing her a five-dollar bill and the corner of newspaper page with a phone number on it, "to let me know if he comes around."

She reports that Ashbless drove off toward the west in an old pickup truck with a two-by-four bumper decorated with painted palm trees on either side of the word "Kahuna." Our follow-up phone call found Ms. Sessions somewhat more articulate but apparently terrified. She now denied that Ashbless had said anything about road apples, but might have used the word "apple-john" instead, although neither of the two terms seemed to make good sense to her. To our minds, whether the small man's face had the appearance of a road apple or an apple-john, the result is equally problematic.

That second phone call was abruptly terminated, and the following day there was a brief article in the Press Telegram about a garage fire in Hawaiian Gardens that was, as usual, blamed on faulty wiring. No one, thank God, was injured. The address was that of the home of Ida Sessions…

The telephone number on the slip of newspaper turned out to be the payphone at Egg Heaven out in Long Beach, where Ashbless had been briefly employed washing dishes, although he gave notice, the manager tells us, on the day of the Hawaiian Gardens fire and hadn't been seen since. We were apparently the third party to inquire about Ashbless in two days' time. The first was our reporter friend Bill Wylie and the second was, according to our contact at Egg Heaven, “a small man with dead-white hair who looked like a goddamn mummy. You wouldn’t call him a midget,” said our contact, “at least not to his face.”

Mr. Wylie, hoping to finish the interrupted interview and recover his forty dollars, walked from Egg Heaven up to Ashbless’s Long Beach apartment on Ximeno Street, but found that the apartment is not only locked, but the doors and windows are screwed shut. Further inquiries led him to Mr. Blaylock’s house in the city of Orange, where Blaylock and Powers were holding a yard sale. “They sold me a bale of what they told me was alpaca fur for fifty bucks,” Wylie told Subterranean Press, evidently irritated. “They said it was worth five hundred dollars at the Old Weaver Craft House in La Mirada.” The “alpaca fur” turned out to be a bale of shredded newspaper packed in hair from some kind of white dog.

It's possible that we give these events more elaboration here than they're worth. It's hard to tell. But in the interest of truth, which is always our highest priority, we'll reveal that there is no "Old Weaver Craft House" in La Mirada. Powers and Blaylock aren't available for comment, and neither, of course, is Ashbless. We paid Mr. Wylie ninety dollars as a flat fee for this "interview," so aside from gas money and a large helping of frustration, he broke even.

We're reminded of Hemingway's assertion, that freelance reporting is a hard dollar under any circumstances. Sometimes, apparently, it's no kind of dollar at all...

And now we give you our careful transcription of the only known interview of William Ashbless, fragmentary though it is, conducted at Joe Jost's bar on Anaheim Street in August of the year 2007.

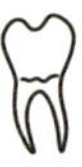

(Wylie's Introductory paragraphs:)

William Ashbless an Interview with the Poet
by Bill Wylie

If you drive up and down Long Beach Boulevard frequently, you've probably noticed the tall, gangly old fellow with the beret and the long white beard, who is generally striding along with an air of stern purpose. Finally overwhelmed by curiosity, your reporter approached the old fellow at Joe Jost's eatery to find out his story. And what a story it is!

His name, apparently, is William Ashbless, and if that name seems to ring a bell with you English Lit majors—well, this old gentleman claims to actually be the minor Regency Period poet of that name, who history tells us was born in 1785 and died in 1846!

"Well I didn't die then," he says gruffly, to anyone who will listen. "Obviously. Another...fellow did, and his body was identified as mine." On this subject he will say no more, scowling and tapping his nose when I inquire.

Very well—then to what does he attribute his remarkable longevity since, ahem, 1846? Magnetism, he says. For the last two hundred years he has worn magnets in his hat, to "keep the iron locked in the blood."

But Ashbless is more concerned with the future these days. There is, it seems, some interest in Hollywood in doing a biopic of his life. "It's an Indie company," he confides. "I believe that means it's being put together by Indians. I have nothing but respect for Indians, and very little of that, but they're letting me write the screenplay for a share of the net, which ought to be huge. I mean to say, if it's Indians casting the net, there's going to be fish in it!" (Laughter from Ashbless) "No money up front though, which is a damn shame." He moves aside a ratty old briefcase and gestures toward what is apparently the "screenplay"—a stack of typed sheets liberally interspersed with paper plates that have tiny handwriting on them. One of the manuscript paper plates has become separated from the stack, and now holds half a dozen pickled eggs and jalapeno peppers...

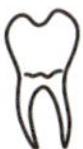

(Wylie's unfinished article ends here. The following is transcribed from his recording.)

ASHBLESS: Try one of these jalapeno eggs, son. They're Jim Dandy.

(Rustling of wax paper, followed by violent coughing.)

ASHBLESS: (apparently to a waiter) Get this man a draft, Jimmy. Put it on his tab, and bring me another round. Make it two.

WYLIE (recovered): A share of the net?

ASHBLESS: Four percent, they tell me. Even if the movie only rakes in ten or twenty million, that's real money to a man like me. Retirement's not an option, you know. Retirement from what? Poetry? They say these Indie films clean house overseas. I'm big in France. The frogs will eat it up. There's an image! Frogs eating up a big guy in France—(pauses to write a note to himself)

WYLIE: Who will they cast for the lead?

ASHBLESS (distracted, still writing): That fellow the cannibal. Wears the damn hockey mask. He was one of the Little Rascals originally.

WYLIE: Anthony Hopkins?

ASHBLESS: That's the one.

WYLIE: I don't think he was—

ASHBLESS: He jumped at the chance, they tell me. Tears in his eyes. There's a love interest, too. I asked for Kate Hepburn. Told them I wouldn't take no.

WYLIE: I believe that Katherine Hepburn passed away some time back…

ASHBLESS: I'm sure you're wrong.

WYLIE (to waiter): You've heard of Katherine Hepburn?

WAITER: Dead actress, right? In *The Sound of Music*? (Waiter clanks down the beers and moves away.)

(Period of silence, then a labored sob.)

WYLIE: Are you all right, sir?

ASHBLESS: They might have told me, the sons of bitches.

WYLIE: Did you know Ms. Hepburn?

ASHBLESS: Know her? What the hell are you suggesting…?

WYLIE: I mean were you acquainted with her.

ASHBLESS: Oh, of course. Yes, I was. That was back at the dawn of time, at least from the point of view of a squeaker like yourself. We had a fistfight back behind Sardi's—

WYLIE: You and Katherine Hepburn?

ASHBLESS: No, you idiot, me and Spencer Tracy. That man could throw a punch, but I cleaned his plow.

WYLIE: You're telling me you fought Spencer Tracy over Katherine Hepburn?

ASHBLESS: Right out there on the sidewalk, bare knuckles. But then she took out after me with her purse and cleared a patch out of my scalp. I felt like a heel for years after that, and I thought I could finally make it up to her by putting her in this picture, and now everybody says she's dead. They're pretty much all of them gone now...

WYLIE: You've seen a lot in your day, haven't you, sir?

ASHBLESS: Son, what I've seen is the world passing away, over and over and over again. "Many a rose-lipped maiden and many a lightfoot lad," as poor old Alfie Housman used to say all the time. For a while I was engaged to a girl who had a wooden leg, but I had to break it off. Every one of 'em's root mulch now. I smoked a cigar with Winnie Churchill on the night they blew up that big Zeppelin. His daddy was a geneticist, you know.

WYLIE: I didn't. I thought...

ASHBLESS: First successful crossbreeding of mammals. Not very many people know that. He crossed a mink with a gorilla. It made a hell of a coat, but the sleeves were too long!

(A long bout of laughter, apparently from Ashbless, followed by desperate, prolonged wheezing.)

WYLIE: Tell me more about the film. What's the focus? The early years?

ASHBLESS (shuffling through his "manuscript"): God knows. It's here in my script somewhere. I've got to hone down about 800 pages before I find out, though, because I've pretty much been putting it all in. These Indian gentlemen I was telling you about want to feature the poetry. If poetry was a boat I'd be Thor Heyerdahl. Make a big old boat like a straw hat out of my paper-plate manuscripts, like his Caltiki...

WYLIE: You might mean Kon Tiki, actually. Caltiki was that Aztec god made out of petroleum products.

ASHBLESS: Aztec, Hasbro —what the hell difference does it make. I'd need a stapler. I'm talking about poetry here, not Vaseline. What's the matter with you?

WYLIE: Where are they intending to film the movie? I gather there are scenes that take place in 19th century London?

ASHBLESS: They're talking about building sets out in Muscoy—that's outside of San Bernardino, below the Cajon Pass. An associate of theirs has a house out there with a big yard, they tell me, and some old broke-down cars that could be dressed up to look like ships. Computer graphics will fix up the details, I imagine.

WYLIE: Doesn't Mr., uh, Powers live out in Muscoy?

ASHBLESS (after a pause, very loud): Swine! Yes! This is them again, Blaylock and Powers! 'No money up front!' No money at all, that's their style! They want me to write a script—! Too cowardly to face me themselves! I'll give those two nitwits a script—I'll do it in pantomime for them, with a baseball bat! I'll—what, what?

JIMMY (the waiter): A man was asking for you. Betty said he looked like the mummy on a good day. She told him you stepped out, but he said your truck was still parked outside, and that he'd take a look up the street and be back in five. Friend of yours?

(The sound of papers being hastily assembled. A glass breaks on the floor. Muttering.)

ASHBLESS: If you can stall him for a couple of minutes, Jimmy, I'd be much obliged. But don't do anything to irritate him! I mean nothing at all. I'll just go out the alley door and find my own way to the street. Mr. Wylie Coyote here will settle the tab.

WYLIE: I guess so. Sure, Mr. Ashbless. Can we...? Is the interview over?

ASHBLESS: I'll catch you another time, Billy. My poor old mother's on the ropes down in Dago. Might not last out the night. If I'm any kind of son I'll be there when she expires. Can you loan me some gas money...? I'm good for it, now that I stand to inherit. Indians! My poetic ass!

WYLIE: I guess so...I've only got forty dollars....

ASHBLESS: Forty should just do the trick, with these jacked-up gas prices. I hate to wipe you out like this, but it's the Christian thing for you to do. You're a good sort, so you know that. God smiles on a generous man. (Inarticulate growl) I'll go and smile on those two weasels.

JIMMY (raised voice): There's the high sign from Betty. He's coming around the corner!

ASHBLESS: Say you don't know me, as you value your life!

(The sound of feet shuffling, a door slamming.)

JIMMY: That'll be twenty-two fifty for the eggs and beer, pal.

WYLIE: I haven't...I mean, I just gave all of my money to Mr. Ashbless...

(Five seconds of vague roaring follow, punctuated by angry shouts and the sound of breaking glass, and then the recorder shuts off, and we're left to our imagination.)